DARK
and other
collected short stories

by Paul Holland

ISBN 978-0-9854972-9-3
Published by:
SWG Group, LLC, Fairfield, NJ

Dedication
To my Rose -
darkness is not a thing
only the absence of a thing
and there is a light
that never fades.

FORWARD

I think that the short story is an ideal vehicle for our time compressed society.

DARK is my third collection of little tales. The first was titled, SHORT and the second MORE PLEASE.

I hope you enjoy them, that they make you think and who knows, perhaps even ask for more (please)…

Table of Contents

ZERO

"How much do you know about zombies?"

Carlson stared at the man across the desk from him, his face frozen for a minute, confused by the question. He was accustomed to dealing with the quirks and oddities of researchers who, he thought, often took delight in vying for the title, "King of the Nerds". Strangely though, Dr. Lewis who occupied the other chair was not like that. He seemed as serious as a heart attack when he tried asking again, "You inquired about my research and I asked you how much you know about zombies?"

Carlson cleared his throat to regain a little composure and said, "Just what one sees in the latest apocalypse film, you know, undead, reanimated creatures running about infecting whatever humans they can't consume outright. Shoot them in the head. I think that pretty much describes the plot, regardless of the title. If not mistaken there is also a mixed drink by that name. I admit I'm confused by your question. It was my understanding that your work was involved in advanced anesthetics."

Lewis pursed his lips, "Your answer is not surprising. I rather expect that would be the response of virtually anyone you stopped on the street given the reach of Hollywood and television. They might not remember the drink though. The concept of the zombie, however, has a basis in reality and that is where our story begins. Historically, different forms of sympathetic magic practitioners would employ natural drugs with potent hypnotic or hallucinogenic properties to create catatonic states. The "Curse of the Zombie" was actually a way of punishing a person, trapping them within the prison of their own mind for a period of time. Not unlike incarcerating them in a brick and mortar jail, but significantly more efficient. There was no need for a building or guards, and no possibility for escape. Because of the hypnotic nature of their state, they would be immune to pain and exhaustion. In addition, they would be open to suggestion permitting their controller to enslave them to perform menial tasks. Naturally, to a superstitious population they would appear to be, un-dead, an explanation that would be promoted by the practitioner in order to consolidate their power through belief and fear."

Carlson smiled, "Thank you, now your question makes sense. I take it you are investigating these different natural drugs."

"Precisely," Lewis continued, "potent, proven, and already tested on a human population. There was actually a good deal of ground work done between 1920 and 1960 but they lacked much of the technology we have today to fill in the gaps and frankly, public opinion due to the proliferation of Hollywood's popularization of the zombie brought an end to what was very promising research."

"That's interesting. So I assume you have been able to parlay that work to accelerate your own. Exactly how does it work and what is the current status of the project?"

Having defused the initial prejudices he anticipated, Lewis settled into his comfort zone of explaining the nuances of the science, "The mechanism of our discovery is by far and away the most fascinating aspect of the technology. Other drugs must be carefully administered based on each patient's criteria such as age, weight, and their state of health because the subject must metabolize the drug. Too little and the effect is insufficient, too much risks an overdose. Once administered, the subject immediately begins to eliminate it from their system. It is a constantly changing platform. Our discovery, which we refer to as Z437, behaves completely differently. Z437 is not the anesthetic; rather it acts as a catalyst which results in two significant differences. The human body, once exposed to the catalyst, manufactures the actual chemicals that induce the catatonic state. For this reason, it is self regulating and limiting. As the subject's

3

metabolism slows down, the body's synthesis of the chemistry slows down. Because Z437 is a catalyst, it is not consumed in the process. As a result, it does not have to be continually re-administered which can cause boomerang effects in the subject. With Z437; the anesthetized state is always stable, because it is regulated by the patient not the doctor. This quality makes Z437 an ideal candidate for use in medically induced coma or even suspended animation. It also has potential application as a truth serum, as it has a remarkable ability to weaken the will of the subject under its influence."

Lewis paused a moment to permit the scope of what he was saying to sink in and then continued, "As to where the project stands, we already have a human subject under test."

Anticipating the reaction of his new chief administrator, Lewis raised a hand to quiet his response, "I assure you that the set of conditions which lead to this turn of events was serendipitous, and not due to any action on our part. It seems that one of our research team was diagnosed in the early stages of a rare genetic disorder similar to fibromyalgia that is unfortunately incurable and results in a lifetime of progressively more painful episodes. She had already experienced several attacks and the prospect of a lifetime spiraling downward in the throes of the disorder must have been unbearable. She returned to the laboratory one evening and self-administered Z437. We discovered her the next day, here in a coma, along with a note explaining what she had done. We promptly administered the antidote."

Carlson, who had been listening intently, broke in, "So there is an antidote for this…"

"Of sorts," replied Lewis, "Once Z437 is in the subject's system we cannot remove it, yet. We can, however, block its action. As long as that agent is in effect, there are no perceivable side effects from the catalyst. However, unlike Z437 the blocker must be continuously provided on a regular basis or the subject will return to a coma state."

Carlson sat back in his chair for the first time, "Alright, I need to think about all this. We need a plan to move forward from here. I don't need to remind you of the potential fallout we can face for unauthorized human experimentation. There are significant liabilities here, self administered or not. Fortunately, this is just an isolated incident…"

"Well, that is not entirely true." Lewis interjected.

Carlson leaded forward again, "What do you mean? Are there others?"

"Not other subjects, but there have been more incidents." Lewis continued, "As I explained Zero's condition is chronic, she will periodically suspend use of the blocking agent and re-enter a coma state to avoid the onset of an attack."

"I'm sorry," Carlson stopped him, "what is this person's name?"

"Her name is Ruth Novak but we refer to her simply as Subject Zero, as it relates to our work. She voluntarily became our first test case, before we were even ready for subject number one.   So, Ruth was dubbed, Zero."   In anticipation of the next logical question, Lewis continued, "She is currently in a Z437 induced coma. She has successfully entered that state and been revived eleven times now.   Each time she has emerged without any apparent negative side effects. Oddly enough, she even retained partial memories of what transpired while she was under."

"I'd like to see her." Carlson announced, standing up.

The researcher struggled a little stiffly to his feet, "You'll have to excuse me, arthritic hip. Have to get it replaced one of these days. Certainly, I'd like you to see our work first hand. Follow me."

Carlson was a big man in his early forties. Despite the suit and tie, he had an air about him that would have seemed more at home on a football field than a boardroom. From the way he moved, he must have been very athletic in his youth but was probably carrying an extra 20 lbs now. Lewis was the more visually striking of the two, rail thin and a good four inches taller than his companion. He was just sixty now, with graying hair and goatee, his gaunt features and huge hands gave him an oddly skeletal appearance. As the elevator doors hissed shut behind them, the tall man turned to his new boss, "I do have some concerns. We do a great deal of work for the military here in this complex. The nature of Z437, because it is a catalyst and not a drug, is such that even a small amount is sufficient to induce the coma state in a large population. I worry that certain people might try to weaponize this."

Carlson gave him an annoyed look and replied somewhat sarcastically, "Doctor, you knew the nature of our facility before you came here. DOD money helps underwrite your paychecks. If you find that so distasteful, why have you been cashing them for the past eight years? Tremendous good can come from your work. You need to stick to the science and let others worry about the rest."

They walked in silence the rest of the way to the lab.

They arrived to find the balance of the research team engaged in the activities of recording and analyzing data that had become routine after so many episodes. The source of that information lay on a recliner in the center of the space where various connections continuously monitored vital signs which barely registered. Subject Zero, Ruth Novak was a competent, young biochemist when a roll of the genetic dice and a resulting fateful decision changed her into the role of human guinea pig. While the other three residents of the lab busied themselves with their normal duties, Lewis and Carlson stood for a moment watching her. She wore a hospital gown and robe. A thin blanket was draped over her. Her skin was drained of color and there was no apparent sign of breathing. Other than the very infrequent blip on a screen, it would have been easy to mistake her for dead.

Without looking away Carlson said, "Bring her out of it."

Lewis shook his head, "We aren't ready to do that yet. Doctor Ho has a few tests left to finish and before we administer the blocking agent we place her in an oxygen tent for an hour while we raise her body temperature. Just some precautions I set in place to help insure the subject's comfort and safety. Besides, while she is in this state, I'd like to demonstrate some of the other characteristics of Z437 I described. For example…"

Doctor Lewis moved to the recliner and said, "Observe…" as he raised one of the subject's arms and released it. It remained suspended as if frozen in place. "You see," he continued, "while under the influence of Z437 the subject will normally default to a waxy catatonic state. One of the side benefits we hope might be derived from working with the catalyst may be insights into schizophrenia. However, the subject is capable of full mobility and highly susceptible to suggestion, watch."

Then, as if controlling a puppet, through a series of carefully constructed commands, Lewis exhibited his control over the subject. After each spoken instruction she would remain frozen until she could process what was required depending on its complexity. By patiently following the protocol, he was able to have Zero lower her arm, sit, stand, and walk three steps as if in a drug laden stupor or trance.

Carlson watched the short demonstration intently with an increasing appreciation for both the quality of work and the potential of the results the lab had produced. It was then Doctor Ho called Lewis over to review some results and the administrator seized the opportunity to examine the subject a little more closely. She simply stood there, seemingly oblivious to his presence. He pinched her hand without any response. She merely continued to stare vacantly out into space and he noticed how cold her skin was to the touch. He stared closely into her lifeless eyes as if trying to see any spark there and finding none muttered to himself, "You are one amazing zombie."

With that Lewis, heading toward the door excitedly called for Carlson to follow him. Throwing a backward glance at Zero still frozen in place, he hurried after the limping researcher. Catching up quickly he asked, "What's up? Why the rush? I was hoping to see her revived."

Lewis caught his breath as they waited for the elevator doors to open. "Later, I need to get to my office to verify these results." He said, brandishing some printed sheets, "She won't be ready for revival for at least another two hours. This is far more interesting. According to Ho's latest tests, titers of Zero's blood show that the levels of Z437 are increasing. Her body is synthesizing the catalyst. We need to confirm this is the case and that the increase, which appears chemically identical, has in fact the same effect as the original compound."

Carlson looked skeptical. "Is that even possible?"

"Oh yes," Lewis replied, "Our bodies, like all living organisms, are complex biochemical factories. For example, prion theory basically suggests that the way BSE, better known as Mad Cow Disease, replicates is not genetic. Protein function is determined not only by their chemical makeup, but also by their shape and configuration. It proposes that existing healthy proteins are distorted, and twisted into diseased ones. There is so much we simply don't understand."

Carlson paced about his lead researcher's office like a caged lion waiting as the data was collated and compared. When Lewis looked up, he smiled and tapping the printouts that sat on his desk said, "Without question, these results support Ho's observations. Now we need to craft some tests to determine the affectivity of this second generation catalyst..."

Before he could continue, a very disheveled Doctor Ho walked in, unannounced. Indignantly, Lewis looked at his associate. "What happened to you?"

Ho slumped into a chair as though exhausted, "I can't explain it. A few minutes after you left, Zero went crazy, completely feral. We tried to get back onto the recliner but she fought back, kicking, biting and scratching us. Look at my hands." He said, holding them up, "She torn out her IV so we couldn't administer the blocking agent. We finally retreated from the lab, locking her in there. There was nothing else we could do. We'll need a couple of the security guards to help subdue her until we can inject her. I just can't understand what happened."

Lewis looked shocked and incredulous, "Well then, get hold of security and get back there before she wrecks the lab."

Ho rose stiffly to his feet, "I'll get back there now. Could you please call and have security meet me there." As he was leaving, Lewis was already on the phone. When he finished he looked up at Carlson who was standing stock still, mumbling to himself.

As if struck by a realization, suddenly the administrator turned and looked at the older man, "You said it yourself, about Hollywood and TV conditioning our perceptions... and you said she was highly susceptible to suggestion... I may have said something..."

With that the phone rang and Lewis snatched it up.

"Hey Doc, this is security. We found Doctor Ho collapsed on the elevator. We thought he was dead but then he got up and started attacking us. We had to handcuff and gag him to make him stop biting us. I don't know what the hell is going on, but you better get down here."

BACK

The flash was not merely blinding, if exposed to it unprotected it would have been devastating. Even safe within the confines of the laboratory witnessing it remotely through shielded video, system ignition was overpowering. Despite the best efforts of the ventilation system the burning effects of ozone that permeated the air were unmistakable.

So were the results. There on the monitors, which showed the platform from 6 different angles, the senator and his small entourage had vanished in the blink of an eye.

"Amazing, professor…" the balding, little man in the charcoal grey suit said when he could recover sufficiently to speak, "If I hadn't seen it with my own two eyes I never would have believed it. Forgive me but exactly where… I mean when, did they go?"

Dr. Abanee looked up from the array of monitors that were simultaneously streaming a host of data feeds, "I'm sorry you asked a question I think. I was a little preoccupied. What was it you wanted to know?"

Somewhat apologetically, the Senator's remaining aide began again, "I am sorry, I am certain you have a million more important concerns at the moment but I was wonder exactly what time they traveled to, you see the Senator never actually confided in me precisely the nature of his destination. Was it in the future or the past? I really have no clue?"

The scientist tapped several keys, minimizing or shutting down the majority of screens that were running around his workstation and swiveled around to face the bureaucrat and his questions. Leaning back comfortably, he smiled and chuckled as if all the cares in the world were suddenly lifted from his shoulders. "Let me set your mind at ease, I'm sorry but I don't remember your name. So many people came in the Senator and now it would seem it's just you and I."

"Brown, Silas Brown." came the reply.

"Well, Mr. Brown, first off it would be impossible to travel into the future. You could only ever travel into the past."

Brown nervously stroked his eyebrow and looked somewhat confused, "I am not certain I understand. Why not?"

"It is a simple principle of quantum physics... Are you familiar with Schrödinger's cat?" Abanee asked.

Trying to look anywhere and everywhere except into that serenely smiling face, Brown replied,"Somehow simple and quantum physics are two terms I wouldn't expect to use in the same sentence."

Abanee laughed out loud, "Touché let me explain then if I may. Schrödinger's cat was an experiment of the mind. It goes like this. A cat is placed into a sealed box with an infernal device. The device senses radiation from an isotope that will spontaneously decay at some point in time that is impossible to predict. When it senses this radiation – the device will release a poisonous gas that will kill the cat but an observer outside the closed box has absolutely no idea when this might occur. Since there is an equal likelihood that the cat may be alive or dead – in quantum physics, it is <u>both</u> alive and dead simultaneously."

Brown sat simply staring now at his grinning companion, "I have absolutely no idea what you are talking about or how it applies to the Senator."

Abanee laughed again, "Fair enough, let's try this. There is only one past. History is history. The future however is malleable. Depending on countless variables, the future can turn in an infinite number of different directions. All of these possible futures co-exist with equal probability until only one of them becomes the present."

Brown scowled as if deep in thought and countered, "So, if I understand you correctly, history is fixed. Every day and date is a singular target but because it hasn't happened yet the future is just a mass of possibilities..."

Abanee's wry smile never waivered, "Precisely. That is a good way of putting it."

Brown felt himself being drawn into very unfamiliar ground but couldn't help from asking the next logical question. "Well, if you went forward in time then couldn't you just kind of, pick one?"

"The problem would be the intervening history it would create between that point and this one. It would rend the very fabric of time itself because that gap between the two points would be comprised of all possible historical pathways between the present when you departed and the point you arrived – your new present time. So for example; if you left today and journeyed 20 years into the future in a single leap, that intervening twenty years would simultaneously contain any and all combinations of war, peace, prosperity, disease, disaster or economic collapse... all of it. The city of Boston could have burned to the ground or not between now and the new future you have traveled to, a future in which both events will have occurred in your new history. It is an impossible scenario."

The scientist saw the dazed and confused look in the bureaucrat's face, sighed and tried again, "If I asked you to get in a car and travel from New York to San Francisco, you would make choices to take this road or that highway, to stop for gas in this town or the next one. When you reached your destination you could relate an exact history of how you got there. But what if you traveled through time instead from your departure in New York to the point of your arrival in San Francisco. The history of your actual trip would be comprised of all the possible permutations between those two points in time. You would have taken every conceivable roadway and turn because all would exist in equal probability. You would have arrived without incident. You would also have arrived having had breakdowns, flat tires and accidents because the history linking the two events would never actually have happened."

Brown felt his head spinning, "But would that really matter? I mean, if you traveled to the future just to observe and return to our time, why would that lapse in history make a difference?"

"Simple," Abanee's smile returned, "You would not have arrived in the future, because the future is not a place − it is a possibility. You would have arrived in what would be for you and the rest of the universe, the present, which happens to be at a future point in time. However the present, that is say today can only exist built upon a foundation of all our yesterdays that brought us here. In short in the absence of our history, today would not exist. For that reason all of the possible future TODAYS cannot exist because their historical pathway doesn't exist, yet."

Brown sat quietly trying to assimilate all this for a minute, "So if it is impossible to travel into the future, then they must have journeyed into the past."

"So it would appear." Abanee motioned toward the transfer chamber that lay just beyond the interlocked doors to his left.

"I'm serious," Brown snapped. His frustration was growing fueled by what he perceived as the scientist's smug attitude and evasive answers, "I want to know exactly when and where the senator and his party are right now."

Abanee's mood sobered in response to the other man's growing annoyance. "Sadly, I cannot tell you exactly. It was the Senator himself who insisted on punching in his desired coordinates. I can say in general that he was interested in traveling within the last century but beyond that I really don't know."

"Alright then," Brown's anger was bubbling to the surface, "exactly when will they be returning."

"Oh, I'm sorry. I thought I made that clear. They are never coming back."

The aide's jaw dropped. "What do you mean they are never coming back?"

"Well, returning would require that they time travel into the future and as I just explained, that is impossible." Abanee looked confused at the question.

Brown shook his head, "But they wouldn't be traveling into the future. They would just be returning here to the present."

"No, no – it doesn't work that way. Where ever they arrive is their present day and all possible futures exist once more because they have altered the past simply by being there. Even if they attempt not to interfere or change anything, their very existence alters conditions. They consume food and water, they breathe the air. Their bodies emit heat. They carry microbes. They interact with people. They have mass. No matter how hard they try not to, they cannot avoid changing conditions. QED: The past is no longer the same, the intervening historical record no longer exists. No way home."

Brown felt himself fighting back waves of panic. A Senator, his boss, had vanished into the past never to return. How would he ever explain this? It was a public relations nightmare. Hell, it was a punishable offense.   He could go to jail. No one in their right mind would believe this.

"Wait a minute; did the Senator understand that he could never return?"

Abanee appeared thoughtful as he said, "You know I am really not sure. I explained it of course, just as I did to you but quite honestly I found your boss talked very loud and very fast and I don't think he was a very good listener..."

Brown buried his face in his hands, growing nauseous, "Oh my God, what am I going to do. We have to call the authorities, there will be an investigation. I can't go to jail..." His heart was pounding now and he was finding it difficult to breathe when he heard the scientist speaking to him calmly and serenely.

"It is alright, everything is fine.   First, this is a secure, top secret facility.   No one is going to call the authorities, we are the authorities. There won't be any investigation and nobody is going to jail. Relax. In fact, if I understand the situation, didn't your boss leave you in charge until his return, Senator Brown?"

The little bureaucrat suddenly sat upright as if someone had slapped him awake. "What did you call me?"

Abanee's smile had returned, "Why Senator Brown, of course. It would seem that you are the last man standing so to speak, tasked with maintaining the office until your predecessor's return - which you and I know cannot happen."

"I hadn't thought of that," Brown's composure was rapidly returning, "but of course I would have to carry on in his absence. We can't permit circumstances to interfere with the smooth operation of the office."

Abanee settled back comfortably in his chair one more. "Of course not. I'm confident that a competent, political insider such as you knows just how to handle a situation surrounding the Senator's absence. Proxy votes, credible stories to satisfy the press and such. Meanwhile, you would be there to insure that your boss's mission and vision continue unabated." He could see the gears turning faster and faster within the bald head of the man in the grey suit.

"Well, you are right of course. We need a smooth transition. Can't do anything that might alarm our constituents unnecessarily."

Abanee nodded, "Well put. Oh, and by the way, just a housekeeping issue. This facility and my work here were coming up for budgeting in the next round of appropriations. That was after all why your predecessor was so anxious to see the transporter work firsthand. I am sure that I can count on your support as someone who has witnessed the remarkable potential of our efforts here. Besides if we were shut down now at this delicate stage of our operations it would raise a great many questions..."

The color drained momentarily from Brown's face, "We can't have that. I can personally attest as to the absolute necessity of your work here. It is vital to national security."

"Thank you, I knew somehow you would understand and you might be interested to learn that another certain politician from the other side of the aisle, a longtime adversary to your old boss is coming next week for a similar demonstration."

Now it was Brown's turn to settle back in his chair, "Is he indeed... I can only imagine that he will be convinced of the importance of this project in a similar fashion." The new Senator leapt to his feet and shook Abanee's hand vigorously as if already campaigning. "Well, sorry I cannot stay but I am certain you can appreciate how much I have to do considering the situation."

The scientist rose as well as one of his assistant's entered from hallway, "I too have a great deal to analyze and prepare. I am glad that you could come and witness the demonstration and I look forward to a long and mutually beneficial relationship."

With that Brown turned on his heel and hurried quickly from the room.

The young man in the lab coat who had just entered looked at his mentor confused, "What did he mean, Doc? You used the transporter, by yourself? I would have come in early to help you..."

"That's okay. I took care of it. One of our friends from Washington along with a few of his people demanded a dog and pony show so I obliged them. They wanted to travel about 80 years into the past. In fact, I asked them to come in when no one else would be around, they love all that secrecy."

Abanee's youthful helper blurted out in shocked surprise, "But you didn't, did you. They can never get back. They'll alter the historical timeline. This could be disastrous."

The scientist shook his head, "You know me better than that, I would never let some self-serving moron and his goon squad run rough shod through history. I simply reset the machinery so that the power wave would disintegrate them. By the way, do you know where the janitor keeps the big vacuum cleaner?"

HEART

It was just under sixteen inches long, like all the rest in the bag. That size enabled Frank to get six blanks from each eight foot length of hickory he hand selected at the mill. Each length had to be perfect. Straight as an arrow with a flawless grain, after all there was no room for error. Then he would turn and sand each blank to precisely the correct dimensions before polishing it until it shone as smooth and hard as an old bone.

Now he stood silently steeling himself for the task at hand, then with one smooth, practiced stroke the hammer slammed the carefully prepared wooden stake into the chest of the body lying quietly before him. There was no way of knowing in advance whether or not they would react when that sharpened shaft of hickory stabbed through their heart. This was the twenty third vampire he had retired. Sometimes they struggled violently. Sometimes they passed quietly without reacting at all. This seemed to be the latter. Frank waited for a minute to make certain and then after gathering his gear, he started for the passage that lead up from the basement room and back to the light of day. He had not gone three steps though before his latest conquest sat up and swiveled to face him, dangling his legs over the edge.

"Going so soon?"

Frank spun around, drawing his Colt 1911 as he did and pointing the .45 pistol at the grinning figure perched half in and half out of the makeshift casket he had been lying in.

The amused figure gestured at the two inch diameter piece of lumber protruding from his chest, "What's this for? Hat rack, possibly..." Laughing softly, he grasped the stake with both hands and with one sharp tug, pulled it from his chest. He made a cursory examination of Frank's handiwork and then tossed it unceremoniously at the other man's feet where it clattered against the concrete. "Please put the gun down. I would think it would be fairly evident by now that I am something you have never seen before. If you start pulling that trigger, you won't kill me but you might force me to kill you, or worse. I'd really just like to talk to you right now. Okay?"

Reluctantly, Frank slowly returned his gun to its holster. "Okay, talk."

"My goodness, you are so angry. Let's put things in perspective here, I mean – who attacked who, while they were sleeping I might add." The man, or what passed for one, with a rather large hole in his chest paused a moment as if waiting for a reply. If he expected one he was disappointed. "I know who you are. Frank Corbett, retired police officer and vampire hunter, extraordinaire. What is the head count now, you must over twenty."

Frank scowled, "You should have been twenty-three and I still don't understand why you aren't."

"That is truly an interesting story, but first – I'd rather talk about you. Now I suppose that this whole vampire hunter thing can have a certain appeal. Let's face it, the thrill of the hunt, the uncertainty, that adrenalin rush... it has to be the ultimate thrill ride. And I understand what drove you to it. After all, you blame a vampire for the death of your wife and child."

Frank glowered darkly at the grinning apparition that sat mocking him, "You killed them." His grip tightened of his bag as he fought the urge to once more reach for the automatic hanging at the ready under his jacket.

As if reading his mind, the vampire leapt from his perch, crossing the distance to Frank and removed the pistol from its holster before he could. He then spun around behind him positioning himself between his would be executioner and the only exit where he nonchalantly made a great show of unloading the weapon before discarding it.

"There, that's better. The best way to avoid temptation is to take it off the table."

It was anger at his own failure more than fear that spoke next, "What do you want from me? Why don't you just kill me now and get it over with?" Frank spat the words at him.

"I told you, I just want to have a chat with you. Relax. Because you came here to kill me, you assume that is the only way this can end, with one or both of us destroyed."

"How else can it end, you monster."

"Man, you are obstinate." The vampire shook his head. "Let's try again, the name's Ferguson and I didn't kill your family. In fact the same vampire that was involved in their deaths was also the one who turned me. So, I could hold a grudge, just like you if I wanted too. But look at what all that anger has done to you. It's no wonder you don't have friends anymore."

Frank couldn't stand it another second. He let out a howl of rage as he rushed the creature swinging wildly, determined to tear him apart or die in the attempt. Ferguson simply stood there, looking bored, not even bothering to block the ceaseless hammering of Corbett until he finally sank back in exhaustion trying to catch his breath.

Ferguson looked at him as if almost embarrassed by the futility of the man's attack.

"Okay, did you get that out of your system? Can we finish our conversation now?" the vampire tried again.

"Quit toying with me." Frank gasped.

"I really wish you could get over yourself. How many times do I have to tell you that I have no intention of harming you in any way, in fact I'm trying to help you?"

Frank felt wave of exhaustion wash through him. "Why?"

Sensing that he was finally ready to listen, Ferguson began again. "The night your wife and daughter were killed in that terrible accident, you have your facts all wrong. You were driving. It was foggy. Suddenly a figure appeared out of nowhere, standing in the middle of the road. At that moment your car was blind-sided by the truck. That vampire wasn't feeding on your family. He was simply drawn to the scent of all that blood. They were killed instantly and you where having a massive heart attack. This is going to sound weird but the blood of the dead and dying tastes awful. I think it has to do with the presence of things like myoglobin and clotting enzymes released by damaged tissue but that is just my theory. Anyway, you were dying, in severe shock. You really didn't have a clear picture of what was going on until you woke up days later in the hospital and even then you were pumped full of drugs. The last vision you had before you passed out was that vampire hovering over your family, but he didn't kill them. The accident did and I don't see you pounding stakes through truck driver's hearts."

Corbett was fighting hard to hold onto his mass of hatred and grief, "I know what I saw."

Ferguson put his hand on the man's shoulder, "No, you don't but you think you do."

"You make it sound like vampires are some benevolent creatures. Is that what you're saying, we're not bad, just misunderstood? How do you know all this about me anyway?"

The vampire chuckled at the outburst, "We are certainly not benevolent, but we aren't evil, either. If we were the bloodthirsty monsters that Hollywood portrays us as – frankly - humanity wouldn't stand a chance. A lion isn't evil when it eats a zebra and people aren't evil when they eat a cow or a chicken... We do what we need to do to survive, it is our nature. I didn't ask to become a vampire. I didn't answer an ad in the newspaper. It wasn't my chosen career path. All things considered I'd rather be able to take a stroll in the sunshine with my old girlfriend but it didn't work out that way. Like most vampires I feed discretely, with minimal harm to my hosts. I practice safe-feeding so I don't infect them because I don't want what almost happened here. We try not to draw attention to ourselves as a rule. Mistakes happen and sometimes you get more vampires as a result, kind of like teen pregnancy... but with modern technology and big brother watching everywhere you can't just swoop into a village doing your Bela Lugosi impersonation."

Corbett almost felt sorry for the creature, "You still haven't answered my question, and how do you know so much about me, about what happened that night?"

"Well, a couple of reasons," Ferguson continued, "first I told you the vampire you saw that night was the same one that turned me, so much of the story comes straight from the horse's mouth, so to speak. Beyond the fact that they were dead or dying, the reason why he wasn't interested in any of the accident victims was because he had just finished feeding, on me. In fact, I think it was being surprised by the headlights that may have caused him to get a little sloppy and as a result, I wound up infected. Anyway, you and I shared an ambulance ride that night. Obviously, I didn't make it but you did. By an odd quirk of fate, it turns out that I was your ideal donor, so they harvested my heart and put it in you."

Frank's jaw dropped as he involuntarily reached to feel the scar that lay beneath his shirt.

"That's why you couldn't drive a stake through my heart; it isn't where you thought it should be. That's why I have no interest in hurting you. That's why you are so good at sniffing out my kind."

With that Ferguson reached down, recovered the stake lying on the floor and offered it to Corbett who stared at it numbly, "So if you are still interested in killing me, I guess you know where you need to put that now. Of course I not certain if it will work, so the question is; how anxious are you to find out?"

STORY

"It is just a story, really." The old man lying in the bed propped up by pillows began, "Simply a tale to amuse you and make you think."

Carl turned to a more comfortable angle in his chair to watch his great uncle. The man reclining on the bed in front of him was his last remaining relative now that his parents were gone. It was a senseless accident caused by a drunk driver that had taken them from him. Several years before, just after his graduation from college he had promised his father that he would take over the practice of visiting Uncle George if anything happened to him. Naturally Carl had agreed never thinking that the old gentleman might outlive his parents. He was after all much older than they were, although remarkably well preserved. In fact, up until this past year when his great uncle fell ill, a stranger might have thought that George was his father's brother rather than his uncle.

When it all first happened, Carl had resented his promise. In the wake of such a devastating loss, he thought having to look in on George would prove a burden but exactly the opposite had occurred. George shared his love of science and despite his years, Carl was constantly amazed at how he kept up with the headlong advance of technology. Rather than slowing down, the old man's thirst for knowledge was insatiable. He subscribed to and read a host of different scientific journals and was well versed in a half dozen disciplines. Moreover, he was a wealth of history and relationships that spanned to globe. He had grown up in the technology boom that followed World War II and seemed to be on a first name basis with the movers and shakers that had brought it about. What started out as obligation rapidly became anticipation, as his respect and affection for his last living relative grew.

Then came the diagnosis and once more Carl faced the prospect of losing that connection. It was crushing.

"I'm sorry Uncle, I was just lost in thought." Carl forced a smile.

"That's good, to be lost in thought. Most people are lost in the vacuum created by a lack of it." George permitted himself a chuckle, "But I do have a story that I wanted to share with you. One that I know you will appreciate, your father did..."

George was racked by that same dry cough that overtook him sometimes now. When it abated, he took a few sips from the glass of ice water that sat on the nightstand, close at hand.

"It was toward the close of the war, the allies were closing in on Germany and despite last ditch efforts like the Watch on the Rhine, what Americans call the Battle of the Bulge, the handwriting was on the wall. It was only a question of time before Hitler and his cronies fell. After all, their resources were almost exhausted, their production capability in a shambles – in the end all wars are a study in attrition and there was no way they could match the output of the United States and the Soviet Union. Still they had one powerful asset that was in full vigor, a core of intellectual talent that was staggering. I'm talking about some of the world's most brilliant minds in metallurgy, engineering, chemistry, biology, physics, aeronautics, electronics… every discipline, fueled by years of almost limitless access to the resources of one of the world's most powerful industrial military complexes to do research."

Carl shook his head, "But the Nazis were monsters…"

George nodded thoughtfully, "I doubt any sane person would argue with that, but I am not talking about Nazis. I am talking about scientists and engineers. Not the crazy, fringe element doing God knows what in the name of science, every country has those. For the purpose of our story here, we can assume that these were otherwise good people caught up in a world gone mad. For them it was not about nationalism, it was about the work. Flag waving was for the masses, their loyalty was to physics. They knew Hitler was insane and his cause was doomed long before the government could admit it. It was apparent as early as 1940 when Russia took Lithuania, Latvia and Estonia that a battle with the Soviets would be inevitable. Roosevelt and Churchill were collaborating long before the US officially entered the war. But in our story, our little band of scientists were trapped. They were watched like hawks, the government would certainly not permit them to leave, which left them with nothing to do but the work and to plan."

George stopped to rest again for a minute, while Carl sat quietly and patiently watching over him until he began again.

"Still what to do? It was fairly evident, particularly toward the end of the war that they would fall into the hands of either the east or the west. Given the choice, the prospect of going with the Americans seemed infinitely preferable, but in order to make that happen they needed a powerful bargaining chip. That is where fate steps in and our little story takes a fascinating twist. The leader of this little band had long known and used the power of his influence and connections to coordinate the activities of group. He also had established connections that ranged internationally and reached beyond intellectual circles into the arenas of military intelligence and diplomacy. After all, periodically, such organizations needed a technical opinion on information they were gathering. It was through these exchanges that he learned of the now famous Manhattan Project on the part of the United States to build the first atomic bomb. He also learned that, based on the information that had been leaked, it was a project doomed to fail. They were running down the wrong path. He knew this because his little band of geniuses had already built the bomb. In fact they had built three of them."

Carl shook his head, "Are you telling me that Germany had the bomb? That's ridiculous. They would have used it."

George chuckled, "Yes, they would have used it. If they knew it existed, but by that time Germany no longer had a delivery system to make its deployment practical. The airfields, factories, hangers and launch pads were in a shambles. You are right, they were crazy enough to have used them but they would have been land delivered, detonated on local soil. It would have been an act of madness and given the track record of what passed for leadership at that time mushroom clouds and lingering death would have been the inevitable outcome. However in the story, our little band of researchers and their leader saw a much better way to employ them and through certain backdoor channels they reached out to the Americans and the Japanese."

"Wait, they contacted the Japanese... Now I am really confused." Carl said.

"Oh, I think it will all make sense very shortly," George smiled enigmatically, "As the end of the war approached, the Japanese had developed and built a number of huge submarines which would be needed for transportation, particularly since one of their characteristics was a stealth technology to assist in evading detection by sonar. They were designed specifically as submersible aircraft carriers to carry out raids on the Pacific coast of the US in a last desperate attempt to cause disruption and panic. As in the case of Germany, it was too little, too late. They too had exhausted their ability to make war. However, these subs had been developed and were controlled by another elite core of intellectual talent that had, for years, been sharing with their counterpart in Germany. Together they struck a deal."

Carl could not believe what he was hearing, "Are you telling me that the Japanese conspired to drop German made atomic bombs on their own people..."

"Of course." George said, delighted that the young man had grasped it right off, "It was the only scenario that made sense. With the failure of the Manhattan Project, the US was at least another year away from successfully completing their own bomb. An invasion of the Japanese homeland would have proven a blood bath for both sides and the Americans and Japanese knew it. The only way to avoid it was to surrender, which they could not do, except in the aftermath of Hiroshima and Nagasaki. Naturally, the price of those of those bombs was the safe passage and new identities for those core groups of scientists. The bonus of course for the Americans was keeping them out of the hands of the Russians and adding them to their own brain trust."

Carl's head was whirling, "You can't be serious about all this."

The old gentleman laughed, "Of course not, I told you – it is all just a story I made up to amuse you, but I had you going, didn't I?"

"It sounds crazy enough to be true, I will give you that." Carl replied, "But I don't see how anyone could be complicit in dropping nuclear weapons on their own country."

"You trust your politicians entirely too much. Churchill allowed Coventry to be bombed without warning the inhabitants rather than alert Germany that the British government was in possession of an enigma device. They are all monsters in their own way. Perhaps it was Stalin who put best. He said – the death of a man is a tragedy, the death of a million, a statistic." George fell silent for a moment as if he were disconnected, musing over some unpleasant recollection, "But then I have lived a great deal longer than you, seen things that were better off forgotten. It has left me somewhat jaded, I'm afraid. But look at me, destroying your good mood. I am so very glad that you come to see me, Carl... I cherish the time we have been able to spend together. I don't know how much longer we will have for these chats of ours."

"Uncle George, don't talk like that. You have always been in great health. It is probably just your memories of the war as a boy that you find depressing. I can't imagine what it must have been like as a teenager growing up in occupied Holland. You never talk about it."

"Yes, I had almost forgotten, that too was part of the story... a teenager in Holland. Oh, but Carl, before I forget, I reached out to an old friend and colleague of mine. His name is John Semple. I told him about much of the work you are doing on your doctorate. He was very impressed and that is no small task, he is very well placed in the scientific community."

Carl nodded appreciatively, "I don't know the name. Is he in research?"

"Better yet," George smiled, "He is an investor. He has funded a great many projects over the years but it is not surprising you haven't heard of him. He values his anonymity. If he didn't I'm certain he would be hounded by every crackpot inventor this side of the Mississippi. Make no mistake, he is a genius but his brilliance is in finance and in seeing the possibilities that technology enables."

George sank back comfortably into the pillows and was dozing almost immediately from the exertion of talking so much. Carl simply sat and watched him sleep, mulling over what the old man had been saying. When the day nurse returned, he excused himself and started back to the lab. He had a considerable amount of work that had been piling up there of late. Riding the elevator back down to the lobby, the car stopped and man joined him. They rode in silence for a moment until he turned and said, "Excuse me, but are you related to George van Dien? He lives here in the building."

Carl nodded, "As a matter of fact, yes. He is my great uncle." It was then he took the opportunity to survey the other fellow. He had snow white hair and light blue eyes, like a husky. Impeccably dressed, he had the posture and bearing of someone used to being in charge of the situation, regardless of what that might entail.

"I thought you looked familiar, there is a strong family resemblance. I have known George for a very long time. Wonderful fellow, brilliant engineer, I could tell you some stories. You must be Carl, then. He has told me a great deal about you. He is very proud of you and with good cause if half of what he related about your work is true. Nanotechnology I believe."

Carl silently nodded.

"My name is Semple, John Semple. I'm certain we will be great friends, too."

DARK

He opened his eyes.

At least, he thought he did, but the room was as black as pitch. Fumbling about on the night stand for the lamp, he closed his eyes again in anticipation of the stabbing sensation that was sure to follow as he switched on the light. But nothing happened.

Oh, great he thought, the bulb must be burned out. Hands outstretched, he moved gingerly to the wall feeling his way until he found the wall switch for the overhead light and flipped it up.

Nothing happened.

Wonderful. It was then he realized that there was no light at all coming in from the street lights. This was like being dropped into a well. It had to be a black out. At least they would have a good excuse to sleep in the morning. Which made him wonder what time it was? It was so dark the moon must have set and yet it still had to be well before sunrise. He gingerly felt his way back to bed, while managing to only stub his toes twice. Once there he again felt around for the nightstand and opened the drawer where he kept a small flashlight for emergencies, just like this one. But when he switched it on to look at his watch nothing happened. Shaking it vigorously, he tried turning it on and off several times without success and cursed softly. How could the batteries be dead, he had just replaced them last week.

Wait a minute, he <u>had</u> just replaced them last week...

He ventured once more to the window. He could feel the smooth, cool glass, the frame, the latch... pushing it open, and thrusting his head outside he was struck by two things. The first was the absolute absence of all light. There were no car headlights, no stars overhead, nothing as far as the eye could see – or rather as far as it couldn't see. Listening carefully, he realized that the sound was also all wrong. Normally, any hour of the day or night you could hear the traffic noise from the interstate highway which was only about a half mile away. But there was no sound of the cars and trucks that had droned on ceaselessly in the past, none at all. In fact the only thing he could hear was people calling out in the darkness. Softly in the distance, cries for help, cries of anger, frustration, fear... It was all surreal.

He pulled himself back into the room and staggered back to the bed. Fighting back a growing sense of panic, he reached across the bed and gently shook his wife's arm, "Mary, wake up... wake up I need your help."

"What... what is it, Greg? What time is it? Put the light on."

"It is on Mary."

"What are taking about? It's dark, quit fooling around."

"I'm sorry, go back to sleep. We must be having a blackout." His voice trailed off, "I just wanted to make sure."

It didn't matter, Mary was awake now. "Sure of what? I can't even see you." She said as she tried staring into the inky blackness that enveloped them both.

Greg spoke in the direction that her disembodied voice came from, "It sounds crazy but there just seems to something wrong. I mean, we've had blackouts before but I have never seen anything so completely dark, except once when I was a kid. We went on a field trip to a mine that had been converted into a kind of museum tour. When we were underground the guide killed the lights for a minute to give us a taste of real darkness. He warned us first, but nothing could prepare you for that utter blackness. Until I woke you up and you were in the dark too, I was afraid I might have gone blind... I wonder how long this is going to last."

Mary dropped back onto her pillow and pulled the cover around her, "Well, even if they can't restore power, the sun is coming up soon. Put the radio on, if you like. It has a battery backup, maybe you can get some news."

Greg laughed, "I knew there was some reason I married you."

"Yeah," Mary growled into her pillow, "well if you want to stay married you better let me go back to sleep."

Greg resumed his fumbling on the nightstand for the button that controlled the radio and switched it on. As it crackled to life, he quickly reduced the volume to avoid the wrath of his wife who was doing her best to go back to sleep. He just had to remember to reset it or the alarm would never wake them. He listened for the familiar drone of the announcer relating today's news, which always sounded like every other day's news, only to be greeted by static. There wasn't even an emergency broadcast warning. He began to move the dial in the hopes of finding anything other than dead air when he chanced across someone broadcasting from the local community college. She was doing her best to remain calm, while advising others to do the same but the tinge of hysteria that edged her voice was unmistakable. Even though it was quickly apparent that she didn't have any more information than he did, Greg continued to listen for some time simply to hear another human being.   Mary was sound asleep again and having that voice coming out of the darkness was a rock he could anchor to.   Obviously, she was lost in this same blackness.   She kept repeating the telephone number of the station but that was almost hopeless.   He and Mary had long ago gotten rid of their landline phone in favor of wireless, but his cell was in the other room charging.   Trying to reach that was almost impossible when you couldn't see an inch in front of you and he had no idea where Mary had left her phone...

Then he realized, it didn't make any sense.

This couldn't be a blackout.   If it were, the little radio station couldn't be broadcasting, unless they had a generator but if they had a generator, then she would have lights.   It was then he remembered after the last beg storm, it seemed as though half the population had gone out and purchased generators.   Every hardware store and home center was selling them like crazy. They should all be running right now but he couldn't hear one.   When he had looked out the window, there had not been even one glimmer of something running anywhere.

He suddenly felt nauseous, his head was spinning.   He knew that he hadn't gone blind because that would mean that other people like Mary and the girl on the radio must have gone blind simultaneously and that was crazy. There was no way that could happen.

He dropped to the floor and started crawling toward the wall, when he reached it Greg began to work his way through the apartment to the spot where he had plugged in his cell phone before going to bed. Even if it were not fully charged there had to be some life in it.

When he finally reached the wall outlet where he connected it to the charger, he gingerly followed the cord to recover the phone making certain not to drop it. The last thing he needed to do at this point would be to break the screen. Then he sat there staring into the blackness where his hand and the device should be... it had no keys, he couldn't see the screen to dial. Finally fumbling with it, he got it into hands free mode and ordered the phone to dial 911 but the line was busy. At least it was something. Then he remembered the number of the little radio station, the DJ with fear nibbling on the edges of her voice. He asked the phone to dial again and suddenly it was her on the other end of the call. Relief washed over him like a tsunami. After the initial joy of simply finding another human being, they began to share information. There were four people at the station. The girl Sarah, two production engineers, Zach and

Marcia and another student who couldn't sleep and just came down to listen, a fellow named Ray. They had been trying to send out a message to remain calm but they could hear some uproar on the campus. Fortunately because it was a small commuter school, they didn't have a large resident population to deal with but they knew there were students and staff trapped in various buildings and lost on the grounds. They were just about at their wits end, but what more could they do?

Apparently everything was working but everyone had been struck blind, between 2 and 3 o'clock in the morning from what they had been able to piece together.

Greg asked the next logical question, "Do you have any idea what time it is now?"

"I don't know how but Marcia is able to pick up a BBC broadcast so accounting for the time difference we know it almost 8:30 in the morning now." Sarah said.

"That means the sun has been up for a good two hours..." Greg sighed, "That aces it, we are blind I'm afraid." He heard voices in the background, and realized Sarah must have him on speaker.

He though it was Zach who asked, "But how can a population just go blind? It doesn't make any sense."

Another voice that must have been Ray responded, "Back in the 1980's, in Bhopal, India, a chemical plant disaster killed thousands and injured over half a million people. Tens of thousands were blinded."

"Okay but there are no chemical plants around here, nothing blew up at 2 o'clock this morning. We would have heard something." Zach returned sarcastically.

"Stop arguing you two. "Sarah shouted angrily, "You are helping."

Greg said, "She's right. This is bad enough. Let's not make it any worse. If it is some kind of disaster, no matter how big, it isn't going to affect the whole world which help is on the way. We just need to sit tight, keep calm and wait."

"Well, what if it isn't an accident. What if this is some kind of invasion or something?" Zach asked.

Gregg was trying hard to sound relaxed with appearing condescending, "Nobody has the kind of technology. Terrorist groups don't have the ability to pull something like this off and as far as invasion goes, who would want a blind population on their hands? Wouldn't it be easier and faster just to kill us? No, this isn't an invasion."

"You sound like you are trying to convince yourself, man. We aren't sick or injured – we just can't see at the moment. That means that whatever this is probably isn't permanent. As far as nobody having this kind of technology, what you are really saying is – nobody on this planet."

Sarah sighed audibly in disgust, "Please…"

*****

"Well, Doctor, report…" the General said as he strode into the busy command and control module of the mobile field post.

As if on cue, the man in the white lab coat put down the headset he had been listening to incoming reports on and swiveled to face the commander.

"Everything is going precisely as I predicted, sir." He replied smugly, "a few minor incidents, all panic related, but overall the population has been subdued without a shot fired. Blind, they are far more frightened to take a step than to sit still. The monsters in your head are much more terrifying that the ones under the bed."

"I am not amused, doctor. Our response teams are all fully infiltrated and in place by last report. What does our timeline look like currently?"

"They need only wait a short time. Their night vision goggles are worthless because they gather and amplify existing ambient light and there is none. As a result, they must rely exclusively on thermal imaging which is less complete. But heat signatures are outside the range of visible light and as such can be picked up with the appropriate equipment. The gas which we deployed is harmless, odorless and colorless, it simply adsorbs all light in the visible spectrum rendering everyone blind, without doing them any actual harm. The nature of the gas is such that in direct sun, the amount of energy it must adsorb will cause it to heat and expand rapidly, causing it to disperse thermally. The amount of energy it adsorbs will also cause it to degrade rapidly. Those creatures under its sphere of influence will see a gradual brightening beginning within the hour and return to full vision by mid afternoon at the latest, none the worse for the experience. If they follow instructions, your people will be seen as saviors, not soldiers. The rest is a mop up operation."

"Amazing, well done, doctor – almost exactly as you predicted. Is there anything else that we need to do here at the moment?"

"No, but on a personal note, I am going to go get a sandwich and a cup of coffee. Did you want something?"

The Old Man uniformed in his starched and pressed BDUs shook his head, "No, thank you.

The doctor pushed back from the table where he had been seated and stood up, retrieving his cane as he did. Starting out, he recalled it was exactly six steps to the door. Instinctively swinging and tapping the cane before him he remarked sarcastically, "It seems the gas does have one side effect though, it only takes about 12 hours but it turns people into frightened sheep."

COLLISION

"Well, my money is on Wellborne and his team."

"That's because you're a fool. It will never stand up, I have seen Lee's system in operation. This is a done deal."

"Yeah, we'll see about that…"

He heard the argument before turning the corner and hurried a step ahead of the reports to quash the discussion.

Looking sternly at the two technicians involved in their heated discussion, Dr. Eugene Fogerty silenced them with a chopping motion of his hand before the others caught up, "We have visitors. I suggest that if you cannot find a more profitable way to spend your time that I will find it for you. Do I make myself clear?"

They both mumbled an apology and scurried off to escape the annoyed countenance that tracked their steps until they were out of sight.

"Bit of a disagreement, Doc?" Steve Flint asked as he caught up. Of all the reporters, Flint was by far and away the most aggravating. He fancied himself a hard hitting, investigative reporter while the public at large and rest of his professional colleagues considered him little more than a scandal monger, forever looking for the next scandalous sound byte. His reputation as a cutthroat was well-earned and Fogerty had no interest in testing those waters.

"Nothing like that I assure you. You will find however that the intellectual community in general enjoys some good natured banter back and forth. But it is all in the spirit of friendly competition, after all the body of scientific knowledge grows through a process of debate, review and challenge."

Flint looked incredulous, "Right, that must be why those guys sounded like they were on their way to see a couple of middleweights duke it out in a cage match. Did I hear them correctly? Are people betting on this outcome?"

Fogerty bit his tongue and waited for the other reporters to join them. He had learned long ago that it was easier to deal with an aggressive reporter as part of a group than one on one. Alone they could and would be relentless, but in a group setting they had to compete between each other for attention. As such, it was possible to play one off against the other. He made it a point of smiling and waving them on, "Come along, I want to make certain you get to see the test chamber before the actual demonstration so that I can answer some of your questions prior to powering up."

"Thanks for waiting Doctor, you suddenly took off around the corner and I was afraid I might lose you. This facility is gigantic." An overweight, grey haired fellow form one of the wire services remarked.

"Yes, exactly how much farther is it, Doctor Fogerty?" asked a young woman he recognized from a cable news network although he struggled to recall her name.

"We are almost there. In fact it is just through those double doors you see at the end of this corridor." Fogerty smiled.

Continuing on, he led them through the massive shielded doors and into the primary test chamber. The space itself was overwhelming, roughly the size of two football fields, end to end. They we right in the center of it. Stretching away from the middle toward each end were two massive constructs, each being attended by its own swarm of technicians. In the case of the unit to their left, everything seemed to terminate in a single tiny nozzle that pointed directly at the other machine. Its counterpart to the right, followed a similar plan except that it terminated in a tiny plate that directly faced the nozzle.

They stood, transfixed for several minutes taking it all in, watching each of the two teams bustling about, making final corrections, adjustments and checks. Then, Fogerty ushered them into a mezzanine box where they could sit comfortably and observe the demonstration. Once they were all in, he used the time to field and answer their questions regarding the test they were about to witness, taking special care to try and avoid the inquiring Mr. Flint.

"Doctor, can you give us a brief explanation of what we are about to see in terms our viewers will understand?"

Fogerty cleared his throat, "I'll do my best. When people think about our solar system, they envision huge expanses that are empty populated by the sun, planets, moons, asteroids, and so on. People talk about the vacuum of space. But there is actually a great deal more in that void than we realize, I refer to dark matter and dark energy. They are the focus of our experiment today."

"I have heard the terms but I don't really understand what they mean. Frankly it just sounds like science fiction to me."

"Well, certainly Hollywood has latched onto the idea and added the fiction part," Fogerty continued, "but I assure the basis of this is very real. In attempting to resolve the mathematics governing the universe, particularly as it relates to the Big Bang and other theory, theoretical physicists and other researchers found that the numbers just didn't add up, so to speak. If fact, they were way off. The concept of dark matter and dark energy were put forward as a way to explain those discrepancies."

"Are you saying they invented something to make the numbers work, when accountants do that they go to jail..." the room broke into laughter.

Fogerty chuckled too, it was a tough crowd but he expected that. "I know that it might sound that way, but the existence of things is often predicted before their discovery. For example, Pluto was discovered mathematically based on its gravitational affect long before anyone actually saw it. The existence of dark matter was postulated in the same way. Dark energy was a natural extension of that theory in order to balance the process."

"What process?"

"Gravity is a function of mass. Dark matter helps explain the gravitational attractive forces that drove the Big Bang, dark energy helps explain the expansion of the known universe."

"How much dark matter are we talking about?"

"Well," Fogerty said a little pensively, "It has been estimated that about 84.5% of all matter is dark matter and 95.1% of all energy is actually dark energy." He saw fingers typing and pencils scribbling notes.

"So what are we going to see here today?"

This was what Fogerty had been waiting for, "You are here to witness the first true application driven by dark matter and dark energy. We believe that the ability to unleash this will prove to the first sustainable source of effectively unlimited, inexhaustible, safe and affordable power driven by the collision of these two most basic of all forces in the universe."

Another hand shot up, "I really appreciate your efforts to make the clear for our viewers but exactly how does it work?"

"It is based primarily on the work of two men," Fogerty said, "Wellborne, who has been focused on dark energy and Lee who has been a leader in the work with dark matter. They are forces in direct opposition and the collision of these two primal elements will harken back to the origin of our universe itself."

Flint could no longer tolerate being ignored and blurted out, "Sound like the ancient philosophical question of the irresistible force striking the immovable object."

Fogerty looked up, "You know, that is an interesting way of putting it"

Flint continued, "So what is going to happen when they do?"

"I really don't exactly Mr. Flint, but we are about to find out in just about three and a half minutes..."

SWAP

"I'm glad you are finally here, Ned. We really need your help right now."

"What's going on? Where's Harry and what happened to your arm?"

Walter exhaled slowly and forcibly, it seemed no matter what happened Ned never changed. "Okay, let me try to answer in order. We've made a remarkable discovery that we need your help with, Harry is down working in that part of the dig and my arm is fine," he said raising his bandaged hand from the makeshift sling it rested in, "I burned my hand and although it is healing nicely I am trying not to bang it on things. One of the reasons that I need your help in fact is because of the injury. It slows down the progress we can make."

"Okay, fill me in." Ned said.

Walter pointed with his good hand, "We set up a tent and a cot for you. Wouldn't you like to drop your things first?"

Without moving from where he was standing, Ned let the backpack he had slung over one should fall to the ground, "Okay, fill me in."

Shaking his head Walter said, "Fine come have a seat and I'll bring you up to speed."

"Two weeks ago while excavating one of the lower levels Harry noticed a draft coming from what should have been a solid wall. We were 30' below ground level. We spent the next two days just examining and photographing every square inch of that wall. For the most part it exhibited no evidence of being different from the rest of the walls with two exceptions. There was a single inscribed stone set 53" above the floor and there was a single slab measuring 46" x 17" resembling a lintel that was built into the wall at a height of 64". The walls themselves are dry laid indigenous stone, primarily roughhewn granite."

"Tell me about this inscription." Ned was listening intently. It was a skill he possessed, When you had his attention, it was as if nothing else existed in his universe. It could be almost unnerving at times.

"I have never seen characters like this anywhere," Walter produced his tablet computer, "Here is a photograph. At first, we didn't even realize that it was a language. The characters looked more decorative, until we saw the pattern emerge just in the last two days. It is actually written in a ternary code."

"What is a ternary code, I'm not familiar with that?" Ned took the tablet to get a closer look at the lines of circular symbols.

"Computers run on binary code. For example, in a 32 byte system you have 16 pairs of tiny switches, any one of which can be on or off. Those 2 settings, raised to the power of 32 mean you have almost 4.3 million data points to construct a language. A ternary system is based on 3, not 2. If you had a 27 byte ternary system (27 is 3 cubed), you would have over 7.6 trillion permutations with which to construct a language. I should also say that based on the age of the rest of the dig at that level, we estimated the wall was constructed almost 2,800 years ago, that's pretty sophisticated, wouldn't you say?"

Ned studied the photo, zooming in and out on different characters for a minute before handing it back. "Without more there is no way we can ever hope to decipher this."

"We already found our Rosetta stone, I'll get to that." Walter continued, "We systematically dismantled enough of the wall, cataloging each stone, to grant us access to a void beyond. It proved to be an ante chamber measuring 12' x 8'. Naturally we had hoped that it would prove an undisturbed trove of artifacts, however it appeared to be empty with the exception of some pottery shards. We were naturally disappointed but only initially because of what we were about to discover. Harry saw it first and it was a good thing because I almost blundered right into it." He advanced the screen to the next photograph and held up the tablet. Barely visible was a softly shimmering ring, it was little more than a slender disturbance in the air caught in the light of a lantern. "We had no idea what it was at first, but it had only two dimensions. From the side, top or bottom it didn't exist. From the front it is that ring you just saw, from the back it is the same ring but everything that you see through it is a mirror image of what is on the other side. The image was inverted as if flipped by a prism or a lens. I took small stone and tossed it at the ring to see what would happen and it bounced off. At least I thought it did. Then I tried to touch it. As I reached in, my own hand reached back out at me. Here is the video." Again he raised the tablet computer and played the scene recorded as it had happened. "As we were leaving, I again picked my small stone and tossed it once more but this time at the side we had originally thought of as the front. This time it vanished as though it had dropped below the surface of the water. We turned to go, resolved to bring additional equipment, such as we had, the next day to study and record the anomaly when something clattered on the stone by our feet. It was a small crystal, certainly nothing like any of the stone in the surrounding area."

Ned interrupted again, "Where is it now, I'd like to see it."

"Harry has it at the moment with all the other artifacts." Walter said matter of factly.

Ned looked confused by intrigued, "What other artifacts?"

"I'm coming to that. Over the course of the next week we constructed tests to try to learn as much as we could. We shone lights at it from both sides. The back reflected it like a mirror, from the front, the light vanished into the anomaly. Everywhere else the beam was clearly visible on the wall. Videos of all these tests are available for your review of course. Here is where it becomes truly fascinating. At the time there was no immediately apparent response from the anomaly, however as we were leaving I placed my hand," Walter raised his bandaged appendage, "on the wall directly opposite the front of the ring. It was extremely hot but only in that location. Harry and I surmised that the anomaly must be responding to our visible light with infrared. To check this hypothesis, the following day we played music directly in front of the ring. It responded by emitting a range of sounds, here is an audio recording." Walter played an audio file from his computer of a modulating screeching that sounded vaguely metallic.

"Interesting but I don't think it will catch on. You can't dance to it." Ned interjected.

Walter couldn't hide his annoyance, "This is serious..."

Ned was mildly surprised by his old friend's angry response, "Relax, I was trying to lighten the mood a little."

Walter backed down a notch, "I'm sorry it's been a very stressful rollercoaster ride these past two weeks. You have no idea..."

"It's okay, I'm here to help."

"I know, that's why I asked you here." Walter took a deep breath and started again, "The big question was, were these actions just automatic responses or guided by some intelligence? For each of the next 5 days we took one object each day that had been carefully selected as a cultural article that would be inert and non-threatening. They were a wristwatch, a tee shirt, a catalog, a can opener and a small flashlight."

Ned nodded, "Interesting collection."

"Each day one was tossed into the anomaly – here is what came back out." Walter held up the tablet for Ned to see as he spooled slowly through shots of an odd assortment of items. One resembled a kind of harness, another looked like cup or bowl with three compartments, one was a round red ball, the other two defied description.

"Where are the articles themselves? Can I see them?" Ned asked.

"We have been keeping them down by the dig but Harry is bringing them up with him, specifically to show you. He should be here any minute, he's running a little late actually."

Ned sat back rubbing his head, "It is a good thing I know you or I would think this was some kind of elaborate hoax… You mentioned earlier that you had found the key to understanding the inscription, your Rosetta Stone. Any chance I can see it or is Harry bringing that as well?"

"I understand your skepticism. Two weeks ago, if I were sitting where you are I would probably not have been as polite as you have been. The short answer is yes, it is here and you can see it." With that Walter stood up and extracted his hand from the bandage holding it up for him to see. There was a sharp dividing line 3 inches below his wrist. From that point, as cleanly as if I had been attached surgically was an appendage unlike anything he had ever seen. It was pale blue in color covered by skin that looked more reptilian than human, Where fingers had been were three equally spaced digits about 6 inches long, They were flexible and flat, more like flippers than anything else. Walter stood rotating and flexing them to demonstrate their full functionality. "It's odd really. It doesn't feel wrong. In fact, I can't remember when my hand didn't look and work like this it seems so completely natural."

Ned could barely speak, "What happened?" He said transfixed.

"I reached into the anomaly, of course. It was only for a second. When I pulled it back, this was the result." Walter might have been talking about what he had for lunch or a buying a new pair of shoes.

Ned tried to contain his mounting horror, "Why would you do such a thing, are you crazy?"

Seeing his reaction, Walter mercifully slid his hand back into the sling, "Harry was always impatient and utterly fixated on the anomaly. Three days ago, we heard a new sound coming from the ring and before I could stop him, he tried to see what was on the other side. I had to reach in to pull him back." With that they heard the faint echo of footsteps ascending the passageway. "Oh, here he comes now."

WISH

Rick sat at the far end of the bar by himself silently nursing one bourbon after another until the last of the crowd had departed. That was generally the way it worked. On a weekday like this, people had to get up the next morning to go to work. Even the hardcore regulars had called it a night, but Rick showed no signs of moving.

The bartender moved down to that end to check on his sole remaining patron and after watching him quietly for a while said, "You know, I've been around awhile. When I see a guy drinking like you've been doing, he's got a story to tell, maybe more than one."

It seemed like an eternity before Rick finally spoke, "Do I owe you money?"

"No," the bartender shook his head, "Your tab is paid up."

Looking around at the empty bar Rick asked, "Am I bothering anyone?"

"No," the bartender glanced around the quiet room, "there's nobody left here to bother."

Rick nodded slowly and asked quietly, "Then why are you bothering me?"

The bartender just smiled knowingly, "I see, that's the way it is."

Rick returned the man's cordial expression with one that reflected all the bitterness he was choking on, "Yeah, that's the way it is. Give me another one."

The bartender reached behind him and produced a nearly full bottle of Maker's Mark setting it down in front of his surly patron. "I'll make you a deal. Funny thing about bartenders, people will tell you things they wouldn't tell their parish priest or their therapist. I have been around a long, long time. Maybe that's because we're better at keeping a secret and over the course of that I think I have seen or heard just about every dirty trick, underhanded betrayal and hard luck story you can imagine. Probably a lot more you can't. You seem like a nice enough fellow. If you want to chat, I'll listen and you can keep the bottle, on the house."

Rick snorted, unamused, "Sure, why not. But I doubt you have ever heard one like this."

"Try me..." came the response.

Rick downed the remainder of his glass and took a deep breath before beginning. "I was married for 13 years. I had my own small manufacturing company, 18 employees. I worked hard but life was good. Then one day, 3 years ago I had an opportunity. I formed a joint venture with a guy who had been one of my bigger customers and things went along pretty well for about 6 or 8 months, or so I thought. Then I started to lose contracts and bids. Quality and productivity fell off. Then I had some people leave. Parts went missing, scrap rates and costs went up. Everything just kept spiraling downward no matter what I did. Money got tighter and tighter. My wife was just angry all the time. Then in one week, my whole world collapsed."

He stopped long enough to pour himself another from the bottle on the bar before continuing, "It seems my partner was the reason that the business was failing. Not only had he been playing fast and loose with the books, skimming off what little profit there was... He had been pirating stock and people to set himself up in direct competition. He used his knowledge of the business to fix bids, steal customers and contracts. He drained my company and used its resources against me. I had trusted him and he had been playing me from day one. Meanwhile on the home front, my wife had cleaned out all our joint accounts moving everything to other banks in her name. She ran every charge card to the limit, stopped paying the mortgage, utilities, everything. Instead of paying the bills, she was paying her own accounts. Two days after the truth came out about my ex-partner I got served with divorce papers. Her hotshot lawyer had been advising her for quite awhile on how to go about hiding the money and sticking me with the bills. I found out later that she was sleeping with the guy. You want to know the worst part? I was sitting in his office, along with my attorney, who I couldn't afford, when I noticed the miserable bastard was wearing my gold watch. She must have taken it and given it to him. The only thing my father had left me and there it was on his wrist."

The bartender shook his head, "Man, I have to tell you. That is cold. Honestly, I have seen and heard worse, but not in a very long time. So what happens now?"

Rick stared at his glass as if the answer were hiding there, "Now, I declared bankruptcy, shut the company down and went to work for a guy that I wouldn't have even done business with 5 years ago. But at least I am paying my bills. If I am careful with my money, I figure I can repay the people who got burned in the process. It will just take a few years."

"I'm impressed." The bartender said, "You know a lot of people would simply walk away and say to heck with everybody else."

"Yeah, well I never said I was very smart but a lot of the folks who got burned were my workers and vendors. They were depending on me and

I let them down. It will take a while but I have to try to set that right if I can."

The bartender chuckled, "Well this might be your lucky day."

"How do you figure that?" Rick asked.

"What if I told you that I am really a genie?" the bartender smiled.

"You mean like the whole rub the magic lamp thing... Then I would probably say that I have either been drinking far too long or not long enough." came the reply.

"I rather expected that. It's the response I usually get, but it doesn't alter the fact. I'm a genie."

Rick snorted, "Right, then what are you doing tending bar here, oh mighty genie. Moonlighting to make a few extra bucks... I mean, aren't you supposed to be serving the master of the lamp someplace?"

The bartender looked at him sheepishly, "The truth of the matter is that whole lamp thing is a gross exaggeration of the facts. Genies aren't confined to material objects like lamps or rings, but we are bound by very strict rules of conduct. If we weren't, frankly, it could really upset the order of things. You know the old absolute power corrupting absolutely. I'm here because I enjoy meeting people. It breaks up the monotony."

Rick nodded, playing along, "Sure, I can see that, I guess being a genie gets boring..."

"Well, I guess it's like any job, except you can't quit and at times it's frustrating. See, that's kind of the problem I have right now. I'd really like to help you. You seem like a nice guy that just got caught under the wheels of the bus, here's the thing," the bartender paused, "Whenever we grant wishes, they backfire. It's like that short story, *The Monkey's Paw*. We lack the wisdom to know what to wish for and we get trapped in our own devices. I'll give you an example. I had a guy not long ago who thought he was really smart so he didn't wish for immortality. He figured that if it all went bad, he would be stuck with it. So instead he wished to live a healthy life for 1,000 years."

Rick said, "Okay that sounds like a pretty good compromise."

"It does, except that now he is a sequoia in the John Muir Forest. I had another guy about a year ago who wished for 100 million dollars but he thought he could outsmart the process so he added the stipulation that it would be exempt from income tax. The next day his entire house was packed with one million, brand new $100 bills. The kicker was that every one had the same serial number. The IRS didn't care but the Secret Service was all over him for counterfeiting. He'll still be in prison when that sequoia falls down. I remember one guy back in 1969, right after the moon landing. He wished that he could be the first man to set foot on Mars." The bartender chuckled.

Rick looked confused, "NASA never sent anybody to Mars."

"Nope, but when they do, boy, are they going to be surprised."

Rick laughed out loud at last, "Well doesn't that just beat all. I find a genie and I still can't win. That's just my luck all over."

Now the bartender's smile faded, "I'm not an evil genie, although I must admit to getting a certain amount of enjoyment from seeing people get their just desserts. I really am sorry, Rick... I wish there was something I could do but those are the rules. In fact, I'm bending them as is just by warning you about how it works. You are supposed to be surprised, like that guy with the 100 million... I have an idea though. It's entirely up to you. If you want, I'll grant you three wishes. That way, if the first one goes bad and honestly it always goes bad, you at least have two shots to get yourself back out of trouble. What do you say?"

Rick couldn't stop laughing by this point. Something he didn't think he might ever be able to do again. "Sure, what the heck, I'll play along. I've got three wishes, right. Okay, for my first wish I want to give my other two wishes away. One goes to my ex-wife and the other goes to my ex-partner."

The bartender stood there utterly flabbergasted, "That is inspired, it's brilliant. You know in over 8,000 years of granting the ridiculous wishes of greedy, short-sighted people, I thought had seen everything but this is the best, I think I love you, man. This is going to be more fun than I've had in centuries. I'm all tingly, I can hardly wait. I want you to know how much I appreciate this and I'm going to make you proud."

As he watched the bartender seemed to expand and become increasingly translucent for a few seconds, then he popped like a soap bubble leaving only a wisp of smoke behind.

Rick simply stared at the spot where the genie had stood for a few seconds and then called out to the other bartender who was cleaning up at the other end of the bar. "Hey, where did he go?"

"Where did who go?" Came a very tired reply.

"Your buddy, the other bartender."

"There's no other bartender, what are you talking about? I think you've had enough." The other man said gruffly, "You're not driving - I'll call you a cab."

Rick slid off the stool and slapped a twenty dollar bill on the bar. "That's alright, it's a nice night. I think I'll walk. I didn't realize how late it was…" instinctively he glanced at his wrist and to his surprise saw a familiar gleam of gold, "But you know what, I think it's never too late and I have a hunch my luck is about to turn around. Keep the change."

Thrusting his hands in his pockets, he started to whistle as he headed out the door.

SMILE

"You're fired."

Higgins replied calmly, "That was quick at least. I really can't say I'm surprised."

The young man seated behind the desk looked mildly pleased, "Well, you're certainly reacting better than I expected. Thanks for not taking it personally."

Higgins simply stood there leaning over, his hands on the back of the chair he had not even had an opportunity to sit down in before being summarily terminated. "Don't misunderstand, I take it very personally." He said smiling grimly, "I just refuse to behave unprofessionally about the whole thing."

"Good," came the curt response, "I expect you to leave the facility immediately. I'm sure you can appreciate the reasons why that's best. I'll have someone clean out your desk and you can pick up your things tomorrow, the box will be with the receptionist or if you'd rather I'll have them shipped to you. Oh, and I'm sure that I don't need to remind you that you have non-compete and nondisclosure agreements with the company."

Higgins just continued to stand there, his face still contorted into a forced smile. Looking at his former boss he said merely, "No, that won't do."

"I beg your pardon..."

"You should beg my pardon," the older man said, "but you won't. I started with this company when there were just four of us. In fact I was working here more than ten years before you were born."

The man behind the desk sighed impatiently, "So much for being spared any histrionics. Thank you for your long and loyal service. Go enjoy your retirement; I still have work to do today. If you have difficulty finding the door, I can ask security to help you."

"You missed the point." Higgins started again, "You and I have a few minor matters to resolve before anybody goes anywhere. First, no one is going to clean out my desk but me. I'll do that when I am done here and we will be done here when I say so, not you. If don't like that, please call security but they all know me and they won't interfere. If you don't believe me, make the call."

Taggert, the interim CEO placed here by the board to "straighten things out" glared at his former VP. He reached for the phone and thought better of it. That was probably just the kind of incident Higgins would have wanted, "Fine, get your things and get out."

"No, we still have a little misunderstanding to resolve."

Taggert stood up and placing his hands on the desk loomed closer to the older man, "And what exactly is that?"

"Well for example, you mentioned my non-compete and nondisclosure agreements."

"What about them?" Taggert asked angrily.

"There's something I'd like to show you. Would you mind taking them out of my personnel file? It's right there on your desk." Higgins pointed to a manila folder laying atop a stack of papers.

"Very well," Taggert grabbed the file and started rummaging through it thinking anything to get rid of the man at this point. But the documents weren't there. "I'm sorry, they are not here. They must be down at HR."

"No, actually they aren't there either because they don't exist. I never signed any such documents." Higgins beamed.

"That's ridiculous. You had to. Everyone has to..." Taggert stammered.

"Well, they do today but I told you – I started here over forty years ago. Nobody ever thought about such things then. That was because nobody needed them. People just treated each other fairly and honestly. Loyalty was a way of life. Today kids like you think it's a punch line – something you can use to take advantage of people with when you should be valuing them."

"Spare me, here... sign these" Taggert reached into his desk drawer and produced two blank forms.

Higgins gave him a rather confused look, "Why would I sign these papers – what are they?"

"You know what they are. They are the agreements you should have signed years ago." He tapped on the papers angrily.

Higgins raised his hands in mock surprise, "Why should I sign those, I don't work here. You fired me, don't you remember?"

Now Taggert was fuming. "You will sign˙these immediately or..."

"Or what," came the reply, "you'll sue me, for what? Even if you did, think about what you are really saying. In the short time since your uncle convinced the board to install you here, you have managed to lay off two-thirds of the people. We used to be one of the biggest employers in the county, so go ahead and sue me – good luck finding a sympathetic jury. Call the company attorney and George will tell you. You'd be a fool. No wait, I think you already are one."

"How dare you talk to me that way?"

Now Higgins circled around the chair and eased his large frame into the seat, "Wait, it's going to get worse before it gets better. Remember when you ordered me to use some of my vacation time about a year ago. I hadn't taken a day off in over 12 years since Joan died." He mused silently for a few seconds and continued, "You used my absence to auction off a lot of our equipment and moved the production offshore. The average savings you projected was to be 18 to 22% straight to the bottom line if I remember the report. The only problem is that the quality was awful. Our people have exhausted more than that trying to fix material here and in the field. You also managed to lose two major customers in the process. Our warehouse is full of crap bought and paid for that we can't even salvage. So how much did you really save?"

Taggert grabbed the phone to call security and hit their extension number, "You have no idea what you're talking about, and our profits are up by more than 8% already." The phone dropped to a voicemail box and he slammed the receiver down angrily.

"You might be able to convince two of the board members of that malarkey but I think the rest are done listening. You are showing an 8% increase only because the lion share of payroll is gone but you haven't taken the write offs yet for all that scrap and you haven't figured in the future loss in sales. How long do you think you can keep cooking the books? That's the reason for getting rid of me – I know what's really going on... and who's to blame." Higgins said shaking his head slowly.

Taggert punched the extension for security again only to be greeted by voicemail and hung up again, "Listen you..."

"No, I have wasted more than enough time listening to you and I am done being polite. I have watched you run roughshod over some very good people but I couldn't stop you." Higgins good natured smile had faded, "At least I couldn't then."

Taggert had regained his composure, "You still can't you old fool. You may not think so but I have the board where I want them because I am giving them what they want. Since Cooper died, this company is finally getting a chance to enter the 21st century and that doesn't include a dusty, ancient relic like you. I'm the future, face it. I'm three steps ahead of you and have been since I arrived. You are a washed up old has been. You couldn't do anything to stop me while you were here. You certainly won't be able to now that you're living on social security. So sign the papers or don't because with or without your signature if you make a move against me or this company I will tie you up in court for the rest of your miserable life. I'll make you run through every penny you've got, I'll ruin you."

Now it was Higgins turn to smolder. The mention of Jim Cooper's name only served to infuriate him. He knew that his old friend would be turning in his grave if he could see what had been going on. He sat quietly for a minute to regain his composure and then stood up slowly to face his sneering adversary. "So, you think you've won…"

"You know I have. Now get out."

Higgins nodded, "There is one more thing you need to know."

Taggert gave him a look of utter contempt, "There is absolutely nothing you could possibly say that would interest me in the least."

"I wouldn't bet on that," Higgins replied, "You see, I figured out what you were up to a long time ago and I have been doing some planning of my own. After Jim Cooper died and you came on board, I took a few steps as a precaution. I already had a substantial stock position in the company between options that I had accrued over the course of forty years and additional shares I purchased periodically. I think it's important to support the people who support you. Then when Jim died, he was kind enough to leave me some additional preferred stock in his will."

Taggert stopped him, "I don't care how much stock you may have set aside, you can never out vote the entire board by yourself."

"That's true," Higgins conceded, "But I'm not done. You see, I'm also on the best of terms with Jim's heirs and frankly they are not happy at all with your shenanigans. When I explained to them what's been going on, it seems that they don't approve of your leadership of the company either. I have also taken the liberty of staying in touch with a great many old friends who have been forced out of their jobs here by your short-sighted policies. You would probably be amazed at the volume of stock they hold combined. Still it was not enough, as you pointed out, to override the entire board but I still control all their proxies. Which brings me to the operative question; how certain are you that you have the full faith and support of all the board members, other than your uncle, of course?"

Taggert gritted his teeth, "You miserable…"

"Now, now – it is probably still good practice on your part not to antagonize a major stockholder, or don't they teach that at CEO school anymore?" Higgins asked,"I'm glad I seem have your attention at last because you see the person I have to thank for the final nail in your coffin – is you…"

Taggert looked as if Higgins had slapped him, "What are you talking about?"

Higgins laughed, "Since your offshore supply joint venture has failed, the company has to go back into production as fast as possible but you auctioned off all our key equipment. You fired our best workers. In short, you dismantled our ability to manufacture in house. Without that, the company is out of business."

Higgins waited a few seconds for the realization to sink in and then continued, "But I heard about the auction while on my forced vacation and made arrangements to buy it all for pennies on the dollar. It's sitting in storage, being maintained by three of the best darn mechanics this company ever had, that is of course until you fired them. So in order to stay in business, the board was forced to buy everything back from me, at top dollar. Here's where it really gets good. In lieu of cash, I accepted stock and options in trade so I now control in excess of 51% of this company and it gives me great pleasure to tell you that you are fired."

Taggert's jaw dropped, "That's impossible."

"Quite the contrary," Higgins said, "You may have noticed that you haven't received any email this morning. I already alerted IT to shut down all your passwords. The bank has been contacted. You have been removed as a signatory from all accounts and your company credit cards have been cancelled. Please leave them on the desk along with the keys to the company car. The dealership will be by later today to pick up that ridiculous ego mobile. The laptop, your tablet computer and your phone all belong to the company so you can leave them here as well. But don't worry; I'll have somebody clean out your desk and laptop case. We'll send you the box."

The realization was sinking in as Taggert stammered, "How am I even supposed to get home? I live clear on the other side of town; it's got to be twenty miles at least."

Higgins nodded thoughtfully and glanced toward the other man's expensive Italian handmade loafers, "That sounds about right. Can't say I think much of your choice of footwear, but then you are a man who is good at making bad decisions. Look on the bright side, the shortest path will take you right through the center of town. Think of all those nice people you'll meet along the way that used to work here. Maybe one of them will give you a ride. Now put the cards and the keys on the desk or shall I call security..."

Taggert snorted, "They aren't answering the phone, remember."

"They'll answer the phone." Higgins held up his cell phone, "They were simply instructed not to take your call. I didn't want us to be interrupted. Now if I were you, I get going. Looks like rain."

His hands visibly shaking, Taggert drew his wallet and placed his credit cards and the other items on his former desk, then silently hurried out past the gauntlet of eyes that seemed to line his way to the parking lot. Higgins watched him go then turned to look up at the portrait of Jim Cooper, the company's founder that hung on the wall, "How did I do, Jim?"

He couldn't be certain but it almost seemed as if the painting managed a little smile.

About the author:

Paul Holland had the uncommon wisdom to marry his best friend over thirty years ago and together they managed to raise three fine young people.

The rest, is incidental.

*Other works of fiction
by Paul Holland include:*

G
what if the gravitational constant, isn't
(a short novel)

SHORT
and other selected short stories

More Please
and other selected short stories